Wolf Hill

Hidden Gold

Roderick Hunt

Illustrated by Alex Brychta

OXFORD
UNIVERSITY PRESS

OXFORD

UNIVERSITY PRESS

Great Clarendon Street, Oxford, OX2 6DP

Oxford New York

Auckland Bangkok Buenos Aires Cape Town Chennai
Dar es Salaam Delhi Hong Kong Istanbul Karachi Kolkata
Kuala Lumpur Madrid Melbourne Mexico City Mumbai Nairobi
São Paulo Shanghai Singapore Taipei Tokyo Toronto

with an associated company in Berlin

Oxford is a trade mark of Oxford University Press

© text Roderick Hunt 1998
© illustrations Alex Brychta
First Published 1998
Reprinted 1999, 2001
10 9 8 7 6 5 4

ISBN 0 19 918656 1

Printed in Hong Kong

Chapter 1

After school, Andy met up with Kat and Gizmo. They went to play with Loz.

Loz was at her great-grandmother's house. She always went there after school.

On the way they met Najma. She was pulling a roll of carpet along.

'Help me with this,' said Najma. 'It's for the den. My mum said we could have it.'

The den was an air-raid shelter. Loz had found it in Gran's garden. It was like a little room under ground. Loz had found it by accident.

Loz's gran had a rule about the den.

'When you use it,' she said, 'ask me first.'

'This carpet will look good in the den,' said Gizmo.

The den had a secret. They found it because of the carpet.

Chapter 2

Andy helped Loz and Najma with the carpet. It was a bit too big so they had to fold it on one side.

'It looks smart,' said Kat.

'It's not quite right,' said Loz. 'There's a bump in it.'

'It's the brick floor,' said Najma. 'It's not even. The bricks in the middle stand up.'

Kat stamped on the bricks. 'Perhaps we can stamp them down,' she said.

Gizmo helped Kat to stamp. The floor made a hollow sound.

'That's funny,' said Najma. She tapped on the floor by the steps. 'The floor sounds solid here but it sounds hollow in the middle.'

Loz began to tap all over the floor. There was no mistake.

'There's a secret space under the bricks,' she said. 'What do you think it is?'

Chapter 3

Kat and Najma pulled the carpet up. Everyone looked at the floor.

'My dad has a crow bar,' said Gizmo. 'Maybe we can borrow it.'

'We don't need to,' said Loz. 'The bricks are loose. We can pull them up.'

At first they couldn't move the
bricks. Then Loz used a screwdriver.
At last, one of the bricks came out.
After that, the rest came out easily.

Under the bricks was a wooden
board. The board was loose. Beneath
it was a hole.

Gizmo shone a torch into the hole.
Everyone crowded round.

10

'Look!' said Gizmo.

'What is it?' asked Andy. 'Let me see.'

Inside the hole was a tin box. Loz pulled it out and opened it.

'Oh wow!' she said.

The tin was full of coins.

Chapter 4

They took the tin to show Gran.
Everyone sat round the kitchen
table. Gran looked in the tin.

There were twelve coins. They
looked dark and dull. Gran polished
one. It began to shine.

'They're quite old,' said Andy.
'They have dates on them. This one says 1890.'

'Are they valuable?' asked Gizmo.

'I don't know,' said Gran. 'I don't expect so.'

'Why not take them to school?' said Najma. 'Mr Saffrey might know.'

Nan came to take Loz home. She looked at the coins.

'Let me take them,' she said. 'Maybe I can sell them. People collect old coins.'

'What a good idea,' said Gran.

But it wasn't such a good idea after all.

Chapter 5

The next day Loz was excited. She ran to school. Najma was already in the playground.

Loz had two of the old coins. Nan had let her take them to school.

'I can't wait to show them to Mr Saffrey,' said Loz. 'Will you come with me?'

Mr Saffrey looked at the coins.
'These are gold sovereigns, Loz,' he
said. 'Where did you get them?'

Loz told Mr Saffrey about the den.
'We found a tin with twelve coins in
it,' she said. 'It was hidden under the
floor.'

Mr Saffrey gasped. 'Sovereigns are valuable,' he said. 'Make sure you don't lose them!'

'Will you look after them for me?' asked Loz.

So Mr Saffrey locked the two coins in his desk. It was a good thing he did!

Chapter 6

After school, Mr Saffrey gave the coins back to Loz.

'Keep them safe,' he said.

At that moment, Nan came into the playground. She looked pleased.

'Guess what? I've sold the coins,' she said. 'I got fifty pounds for them!'

Loz gave Nan a hug. 'That's wonderful,' she said.

'I want the other two,' said Nan. 'I'm off to sell them as well.'

Mr Saffrey's face went pale. 'Only fifty pounds!' he said. 'That's terrible! Each coin is worth fifty pounds. You should have got five hundred pounds for them.'

'Oh no,' said Nan. She looked upset. 'I didn't know.'

'We must get the coins back,' said Mr Saffrey.

'But I've sold them,' sniffed Nan. 'It's too late.'

'It may not be,' said Mr Saffrey. 'I've got a plan.'

Chapter 7

Mr Saffrey drove the mini-bus into town. He took Nan, Loz and Najma. Miss Teal went, too. On the way, Mr Saffrey told everyone what to do.

Mr Saffrey and Miss Teal waited outside the coin shop. Nan went inside with the girls. Najma had a bag with her.

The woman in the shop smiled.

'I've brought the other two coins,' said Nan. She put them on the counter.

'This is my granddaughter,' she went on. 'She found all the coins. She thinks these two are valuable.'

The woman looked at the sovereigns.

'Oh no,' she said. 'They're just like the others. I'll give you ten pounds. That's all they're worth.'

Nan took the ten pounds. 'Thank you,' she said.

Outside the shop, Najma gave her bag to Miss Teal.

Nan smiled. 'So far, so good,' she said.

Chapter 8

Mr Saffrey and Miss Teal went into the coin shop.

'We collect coins,' said Mr Saffrey. 'Do you have any sovereigns?'

'You're lucky,' said the woman. 'I've got twelve.'

She put Loz's sovereigns on the counter.

Mr Saffrey picked up three. 'How much are they?' he asked.

'Those are very rare,' said the woman. 'Each one is sixty-five pounds.'

'That's too much,' said Mr Saffrey. 'How about fifty pounds each?'

'I'm sorry,' said the woman. 'Sixty pounds each. I can't sell them for less.'

Miss Teal looked at the sovereigns. 'We'll take them all,' she said.

'That will be seven hundred and twenty pounds,' said the woman.

Then Miss Teal opened Najma's bag. She took out a tape recorder.

'I think you should listen to this,' she said.

Chapter 9

'It was a brilliant plan,' said Loz.

Mr Saffrey grinned. He was
pleased it had worked.

'Tell me what happened again,'
said Gran.

'Well,' said Loz. 'We went into the
shop. Najma had the tape recorder.
The woman said the coins weren't
valuable.'

'Then Mr Saffrey and Miss Teal went in,' said Najma. 'The woman told them the coins were worth sixty-five pounds each.'

'Then we played back the tape,' said Miss Teal. 'The woman went as white as a sheet.'

'She gave back all the coins,' said Loz.

'You know what they are worth, now,' said Mr Saffrey. 'You can get a good price for them.'

'Thank you,' said Nan.

'I know one thing we can do with the money,' said Gran. 'We can put an electric light in the den.'

'Great!' said Loz and Najma.

'Let's think about it,' said Nan.

Chapter 10

These coins were
put here by :
Chris Constantine
Kat Wilson
Loz Smith
Matthew Harding
Andy Freeman
Najma Patel

A week later, everyone met in the den. Chris pulled back the carpet and Najma took the bricks out of the floor.

Andy gave Loz a piece of paper. Everyone wrote their own name on it. Loz put the piece of paper in the old coin tin.

Then everyone gave Loz a coin. 'Years from now someone else will find this tin,' said Loz. 'It will have these coins in it. Maybe they will be valuable too.'

'But these coins are not worth much,' said Gizmo.

'Do you think they will be valuable one day?'

'You never know,' said Kat.